The Santa Clock

This book belongs to

_____

The Santa Clock

By Jimmy Badavino
Illustrated by Christie Colangione-B

Badavino Creative Studios

Badavino Creative Studios

Published in The United States through Create Space

The Santa Clock
Written by Jimmy Badavino, 1972-
Illustrated by Christie Colangione-B, 1970-
Summary: A young boy searching for his siblings on Christmas Eve finds a wonderful discovery, reconnecting him with a new belief in Santa's magic.

ISBN 978-1453880685

1. Christmas   2. Santa   3. Children's Fiction

Badavino Creative Studios website address: jimmybadavino.com

Printed in The United States of America
1 3 5 7 8 10 9 6 4 2

First Edition

Designed by Christie Colangione-B

To our three wonderful children,
Gaetana, Sofia, and
Vincenzo.

Love, Mom and Dad

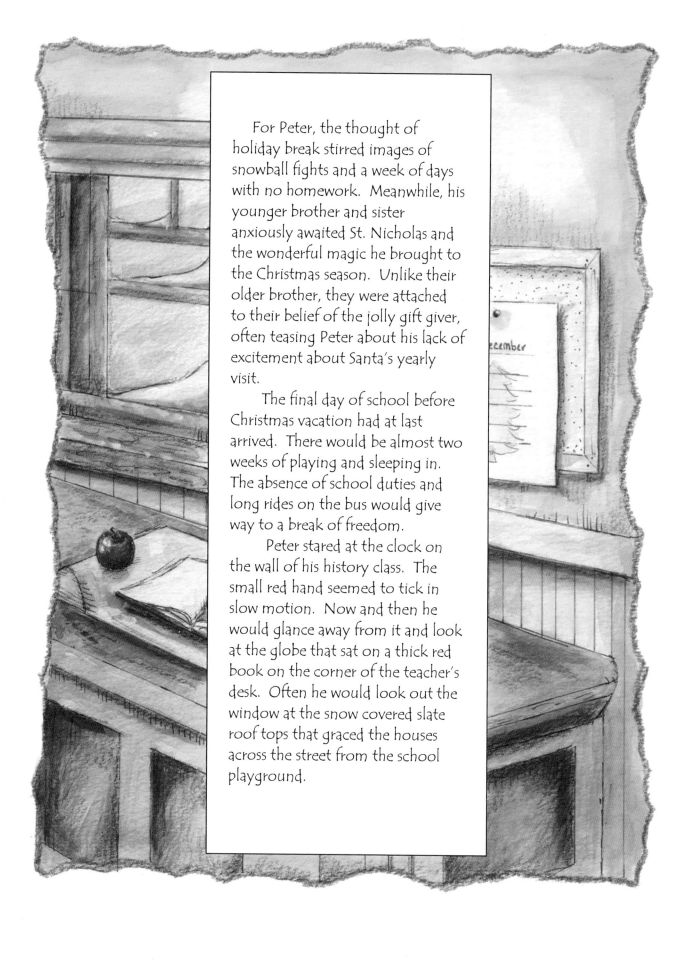

For Peter, the thought of holiday break stirred images of snowball fights and a week of days with no homework. Meanwhile, his younger brother and sister anxiously awaited St. Nicholas and the wonderful magic he brought to the Christmas season. Unlike their older brother, they were attached to their belief of the jolly gift giver, often teasing Peter about his lack of excitement about Santa's yearly visit.

The final day of school before Christmas vacation had at last arrived. There would be almost two weeks of playing and sleeping in. The absence of school duties and long rides on the bus would give way to a break of freedom.

Peter stared at the clock on the wall of his history class. The small red hand seemed to tick in slow motion. Now and then he would glance away from it and look at the globe that sat on a thick red book on the corner of the teacher's desk. Often he would look out the window at the snow covered slate roof tops that graced the houses across the street from the school playground.

Peter would chuckle to himself that his siblings still cherished the stories that he was convinced were impossible. How, he thought to himself as he looked back to the globe, could someone live in some invisible village in the North Pole, and make it around the entire planet delivering gifts to every house, in the same night? Peter remembered forcing himself to stay awake at night to hear a sled and prancing hooves land atop the roof of his family's house, but they never came. He would eventually doze off, and then in the morning he would run down the stairs to feast his eyes upon the filled stockings, and a mountain of gifts under the tree. In the middle of the night, he hadn't heard a thing.

His slumbering eye lids never caught the faint glow across the front lawn of the glaring red light from Santa's lead reindeer. He had sworn he could hear bells jingling, but sometimes thought it was just his imagination.

The year he had given up, Peter had fallen asleep right next to the tree in the family room. When he awoke in the morning, all was typical of a visit from Santa, but he was convinced he would have heard him come down the chimney, or bite into the crunchy cookies that sat on the coffee table. For him, if nobody ever saw Santa Claus putting presents under the tree or filling the stockings, then he must not exist. And of course, he couldn't help but think of how the daunting Christmas Eve task for Santa was just physically impossible to be carried out by one person alone. After that, he looked at it all as a fairy tale, and he no longer held the magic of Christmas spirit as close to his heart as he once had.

When Peter looked back up at the clock, he thought for sure his last fifteen minutes of day dreaming would yield an end of class, and the finish of the school day. But, to his disappointment, only a minute had gone by.

Right up through Christmas Eve, Peter tried to ignore and poke fun at every type of Santa tradition his brother and sister got excited about. This was the first time though that the teasing had raised the spirits of the youngsters so much, that they set out to prove their older brother wrong.

By evening time, Peter began to feel sad about picking on his siblings. When he went upstairs to apologize to his sister, he found a note on her bed that read, "Went to see Santa." He then went to his brother's room where he would stumble upon the same note resting on his pillow. Peter looked around and saw that the dresser drawers had been pulled out and the clothes were rifled through and sloppy. Suddenly it hit him that they must have run off to find proof that he was mistaken in his opinion of Christmas.

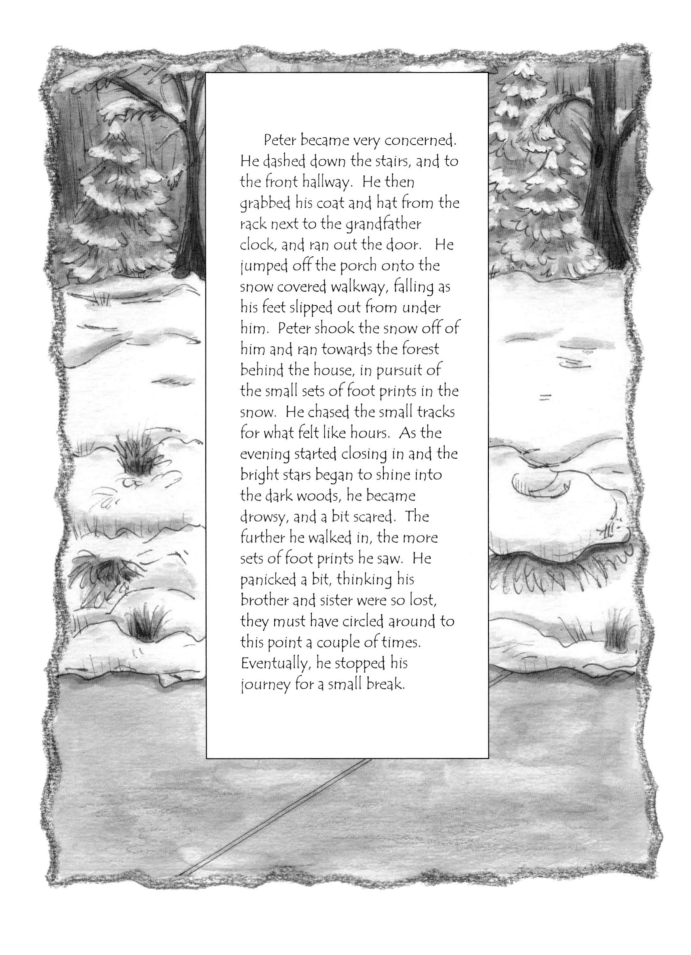

Peter became very concerned. He dashed down the stairs, and to the front hallway. He then grabbed his coat and hat from the rack next to the grandfather clock, and ran out the door. He jumped off the porch onto the snow covered walkway, falling as his feet slipped out from under him. Peter shook the snow off of him and ran towards the forest behind the house, in pursuit of the small sets of foot prints in the snow. He chased the small tracks for what felt like hours. As the evening started closing in and the bright stars began to shine into the dark woods, he became drowsy, and a bit scared. The further he walked in, the more sets of foot prints he saw. He panicked a bit, thinking his brother and sister were so lost, they must have circled around to this point a couple of times. Eventually, he stopped his journey for a small break.

When he sat down, he looked around into the dark forest. Peter was stranded in the middle of nowhere. His concern was still for his brother and sister, but he figured if he waited there a bit, they might come back around to where he was, and then they could follow their foot prints back home.

As a small amount of time went by, Peter asked out loud, "where are they?"

Then, an owl made a noise that sounded more like an answer, "who, who."

"My brother and sister are missing. I have to find them," he said towards the sound of a squeaking squirrel.

A moment later he saw two large deer prancing towards a row of pine trees. "Hey, have you seen them?" he asked.

Peter stood still for a moment. He had just spent a good part of the day teasing his brother and sister for believing in holiday magic, and now he stood in the middle of the forest talking with animals. He convinced himself this must be a strange dream. As he walked behind the large deer, he looked around and saw that many of the small forest creatures were looking at him with curious glares in their eyes. They peaked out from the bushes and stared as he followed the deer towards a faint red light in the distance.

Before he knew it, he was slowly approaching a log cabin, and he saw that the animals that were around him had disappeared. Now he was alone again, in search for his lost brother and sister.

Peter knocked on the front door a few times, but nobody had answered. Finally he pushed on the door and it creaked open. He cautiously entered the house and began to look around. "Hello," he called, searching for a response. Then he stopped as he heard a loud noise. It was a beautiful sound. It was a mystical carol of bells and chimes that made his heart race, drawing his attention towards the room on the opposite side of the cabin.

When he followed the noise into the room, he discovered a beautiful holiday wonderland. Everything was tidy, and the Christmas decorations were bountiful. A train circled overhead around the room while its whistle blew on each pass.

Peter saw a large desk with stacks of papers on the two front corners. He peaked at them and saw that they were names of children from all over the world. Surely he could not be at the North Pole, he thought. He had not traveled that far, and this cabin stood alone by itself in the middle of the woods. There were no signs of elves or toy shops. And, if he were, he wondered, where was Santa Claus?

Suddenly, a large book that sat alone on a small corner cabinet had caught his eye. When he opened it, he realized he was holding something very important. It was a book about Santa and all of his responsibilities to ensure he delivered a Merry Christmas year in and year out. He slowly leafed through the pages and laughed anxiously at each grand task, thinking of how he had just earlier that day argued against all of these things with his brother and sister.

He wasn't sure what to make of the discovery. It actually wasn't much different than many of the stories he grew up loving, but the feel of the book seemed more powerful than that. The book explained how Santa appeared in people's houses and how his magic could make reindeer fly. It told of how Santa could make himself invisible so he could not be seen. But the answer to his biggest question was not in the book. Still he wondered about his ability to get around the world so quickly. As he got to the last page, there was only one sentence that described children who had lost their belief. It simply said, "When the children stop believing in you, they no longer receive gifts through your Christmas magic."

Peter had snooped around for almost an hour when the beautiful melody of the mantle clock began to ring again in the Christmas room. When he turned to look at it though, he saw that it was eleven o'clock, just as it was when he had first entered the room. The clock must be broken, he thought. But the music was so beautiful, it drew him towards it, and as he slowly approached the clock, he noticed something strange. Whenever the second hand made a full circle, the minute hand began to move backwards.

Peter stood and stared at the clock as it continuously did the same thing. Suddenly, he was able to understand the mysterious clock, and then he found an answer to his big question. Santa somehow magically saves time to use for Christmas Eve, he believed. He placed the book back on the table and quickly ran outside. He looked left and right for any signs of his brother and sister, and a moment after that he rushed off, following the foot prints of the children as he headed home. As he chugged his way through the snow, he thought about his day dream on the last day of school before break, and how the clock had barely moved. He remembered the many times a year his parents would say how their day seemed so long, and then he smiled to himself. He envisioned Santa winding the clock back a few minutes here and a few minutes there throughout the year, giving him all the time he needed on Christmas Eve to deliver toys around the world.

He couldn't wait to tell his siblings about his discovery, and he could only hope they had found their way back home. Peter ran again until he couldn't run any more. A slight snow drift had kicked up and made his trek back home harder to accomplish. It became very cold, and the foot prints were beginning to fill back in. He was afraid he would lose his way. When Peter slipped and collapsed into the newly fallen snow, he had heard a loud pinging and knocking sound above him. He peered as hard as he could through the thick flakes and he noticed a bright light shining in the sky.

When he stood up, he saw that he was back in his front yard. The bright light and loud noise was coming from a window up in the attic. Peter then ran quickly into the house and up the stairs to the top floor. When he got there, he saw his younger brother and sister sitting in a large puff of blankets near the window. His brother held a pair of binoculars, and his sister had an oil lamp.

"Where have you two been? I was looking everywhere for you," Peter said, unwrapping his scarf from his neck.

"We came up here to look for Santa tonight," his brother explained.

"Yeah, this is probably the best spot to see him land on the roof top," his sister said.

It came to Peter that his siblings must not have left the house at all, and their dressers were messy from digging out their Christmas pajamas. But what about the prints in the snow, he wondered.

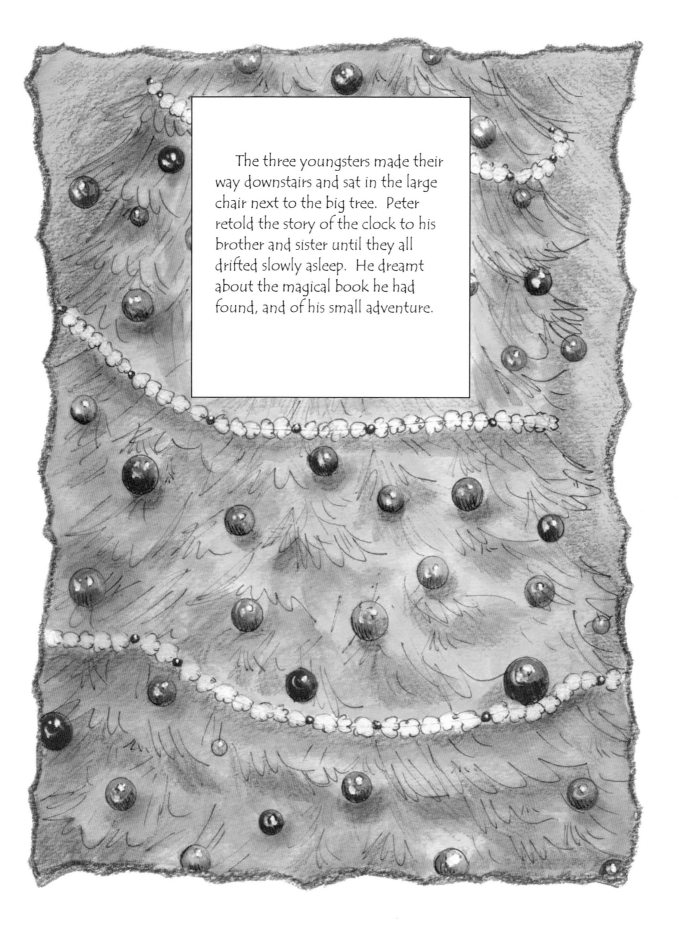

The three youngsters made their way downstairs and sat in the large chair next to the big tree. Peter retold the story of the clock to his brother and sister until they all drifted slowly asleep. He dreamt about the magical book he had found, and of his small adventure.

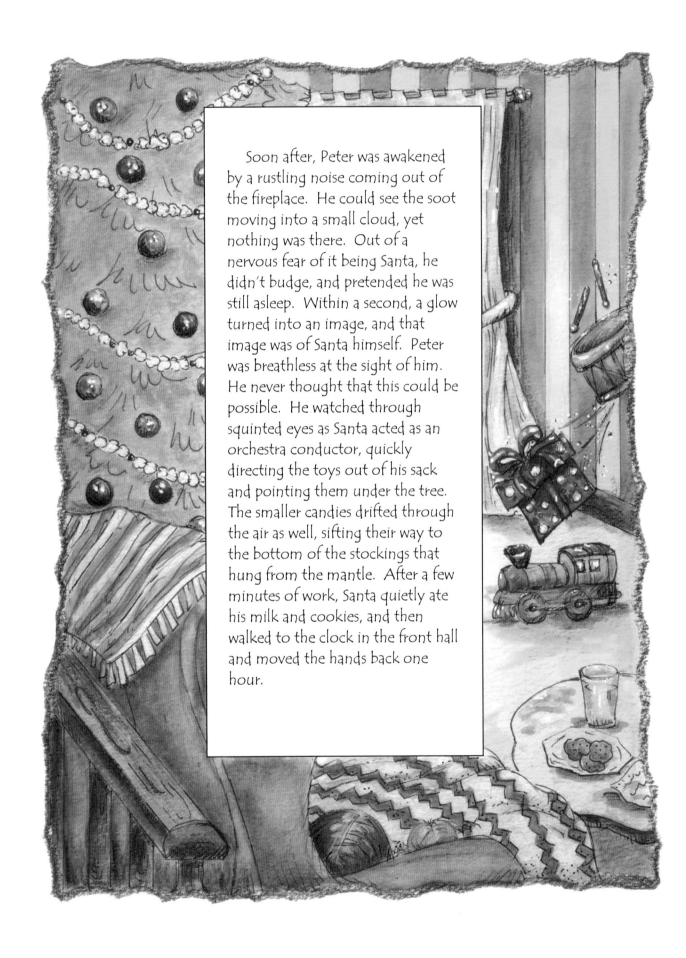

Soon after, Peter was awakened by a rustling noise coming out of the fireplace. He could see the soot moving into a small cloud, yet nothing was there. Out of a nervous fear of it being Santa, he didn't budge, and pretended he was still asleep. Within a second, a glow turned into an image, and that image was of Santa himself. Peter was breathless at the sight of him. He never thought that this could be possible. He watched through squinted eyes as Santa acted as an orchestra conductor, quickly directing the toys out of his sack and pointing them under the tree. The smaller candies drifted through the air as well, sifting their way to the bottom of the stockings that hung from the mantle. After a few minutes of work, Santa quietly ate his milk and cookies, and then walked to the clock in the front hall and moved the hands back one hour.

At last, Peter felt the old elf
approach the chair where he sat with
his slumbering brother and sister.
Santa reached down and lightly
patted the children on their heads.

"Peter, you've given the most
wonderful present to your brother
and sister. The amount of spirit
they keep is up to you," Santa
whispered.

Peter sat up quickly and asked, "Whose trail was I following tonight?"

At that moment, Santa shrunk into a small ball of light and disappeared up the chimney. As the light faded, Peter heard an echo, "Elves," Santa laughed.

He then fell back to sleep and was awakened at six in the morning by the ringing of the grandfather clock in the front hall. Peter smiled, knowing that he had magically slept for more hours than he could imagine, and he laughed to himself, as he realized that every time piece was a Santa clock.

The End

We would like to thank our families for
creating and nurturing holiday traditions
of generations past, present, and future.
-Jimmy and Christie

Thank you Mom and Dad for supporting
my artistic path, and always helping me
focus on blending family and art.
To my husband Jimmy, for helping me
develop the venue to pursue my dreams.
-C.C.B.

Jimmy Badavino was born in Troy, N.Y. He attended Green Mountain College in Vermont, and began his writing career with a published novel in 2009. His love for creative writing led to The Santa Clock, as well as a second novel, a screenplay, and further children's stories that are now in production.

Christie Colangione-B was also born in Troy, and is a graduate of The College of St. Rose in Albany, with a BS in Graphic Design. She is a Designer/Illustrator who has had a life long passion for art. The Santa Clock is her first children's book, and she is currently working on a "Fall themed" story that is due out in 2011.

Jimmy and Christie were married in 1996 and established Badavino Creative Studios in 2009. The unique blend of their talents allows them to share their love of family and tradition with others while creating special moments with their three children.

To purchase more copies, or to find information about other works by Badavino Creative Studios, be sure to visit:
Jimmybadavino.com

Badavino Creative Studios

Made in the USA
Charleston, SC
23 November 2010